KEYSTONES
of the Stone Arch Bridge

KEYSTONES

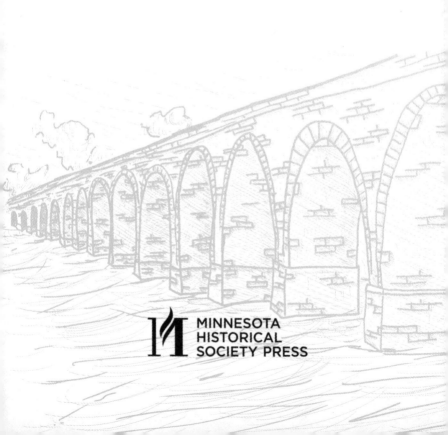

MINNESOTA
HISTORICAL
SOCIETY PRESS

of the
Stone Arch Bridge

Carolyn Ruff

ILLUSTRATIONS BY

Christie Washam

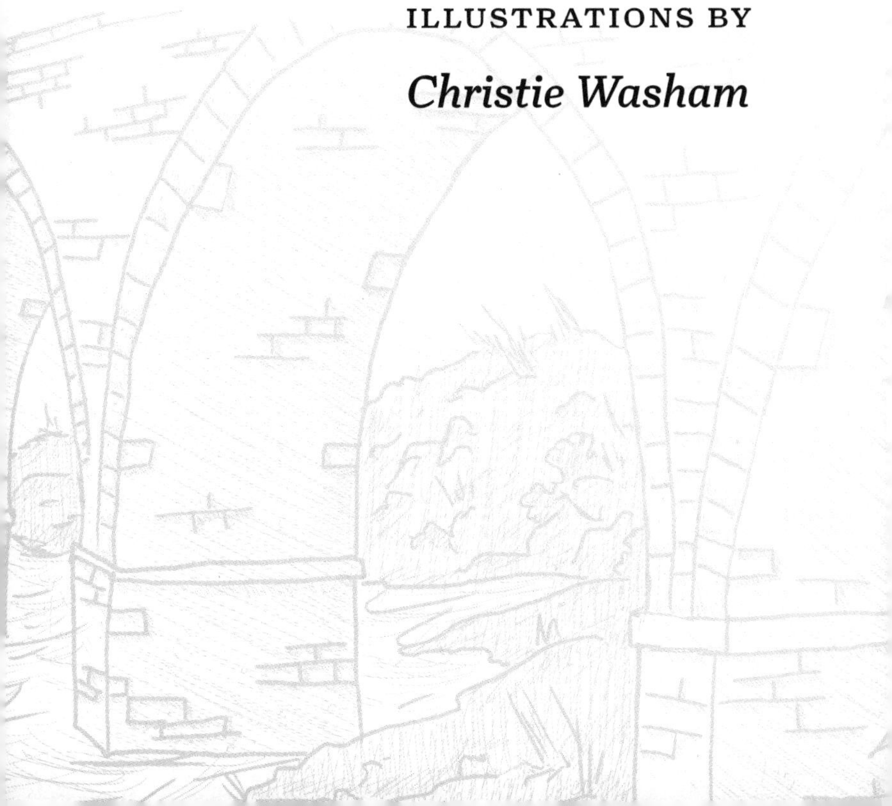

CLEAN
WATER
LAND &
LEGACY
AMENDMENT

www.mhspress.org

The Minnesota Historical Society Press is a member of the Association of American University Presses.

Manufactured in the United States of America

10 9 8 7 6 5 4 3 2 1

♾ The paper used in this publication meets the minimum requirements of the American National Standard for Information Sciences—Permanence for Printed Library Materials, ANSI Z39.48-1984.

International Standard Book Number
ISBN: 978-0-87351-923-6 (paper)
ISBN: 978-0-87351-937-3 (e-book)

Library of Congress Cataloging-in-Publication Data
Ruff, Carolyn.
  Keystones of the Stone Arch Bridge / Carolyn Ruff ; [illustrated by]
  Christie Washam.
      pages cm
  ISBN 978-0-87351-923-6 (pbk. : alk. paper) — ISBN 978-0-87351-937-3 (ebook)
  1. Stone Arch Bridge (Minneapolis, Minn.)—Juvenile literature.
  2. Minneapolis (Minn.)—History—19th century—Juvenile fiction.
  I. Washam, Christie, illustrator. II. Title.
F614.M557.R84 2014
977.6'579—dc23

                                        2013050239

This and other Minnesota Historical Society Press books are available from popular e-book vendors.

Contents

Acknowledgments

I WOULD LIKE TO ACKNOWLEDGE WITH GRATITUDE

the inspiration of classic children's book authors, notably Maurice Sendak, Ezra Jack Keats, and Jean Craighead George, whose stories I shared with innumerable students over the years;

the compelling influence of Joseph Campbell's and Louise Erdrich's writings;

the guidance of teaching artists at the Loft Literary Center, especially Debra Frasier and Mary Casanova;

the support of my colleagues at Mill City Museum, particularly Laura Salveson, Dave Stevens, and Maureen Trepp offered knowledgeable feedback on the many drafts of *Keystones*;

the expertise of my editor at MHS Press, Shannon Pennefeather;

and, of course, the love of my son, Per Jordan, and my daughter, Veronika Lis, who with her husband, Brainerd, recently welcomed twins Beatrix May and Eloise Lillian to our family.

KEYSTONES
of the Stone Arch Bridge

The Fossil

"I GIVE UP, FRITZ. YOU WIN THE HANDSTAND CONTEST," declared Sven as his feet tumbled down from the top of the creaky fence. "Momma's calling me. I better get home."

Fritz could barely smile with all the blood running to his head. His legs wobbled like a newborn colt's, but slowly he stood tall, squared his shoulders, and snapped his suspenders.

"Time for supper!" Sven's mother called from the doorway of their shanty house on the Mississippi River Flats.

"Nils, come along home now," another voice shouted.

"Lise, no dilly-dallying, come and eat," Fritz heard from another direction.

No one called Fritz's name.

Fritz zigzagged along Cooper Street to his gray, wooden house. No need to rush. Poppa wouldn't be home yet from his job as a packer at the flour mill. Once inside, Fritz dove headfirst into the thin, thread-bare quilts on his bed and burrowed down. His cries turned into sobs.

What is Momma doing today back in Sweden? Fritz thought. *Is she making a wild blueberry pie for Hannah and Inge? Momma always gave me the leftover pieces of pie dough sprinkled with cardamom and sugar to eat like cookies warm from the oven. Momma promised, "Vi ses—we'll see each other soon." It's taking so long. I have to find a way to help bring our family to America.*

It was almost dark by the time Poppa came home. They started cooking on the outdoor fireplace built out of river stones and limestone chips from the quarry close by. Poppa moved slowly, but with Fritz's help, the carp and potatoes were finally ready. Poppa muttered to himself as he eased down into his rickety chair at the table.

I've got to come up with a plan, Fritz thought. *I could catch dozens of fish every day and sell them up on Cedar Avenue. Or I could get one of those long sticks with a prong on the end and go out on the platforms that jut into the river. I bet I'd be good at grabbing the wooden blocks, mill ends, and dead heads as they float down from the sawmills. Sometimes the fruit warehouses dump oranges and bananas in the river. They are easy to spot, bobbing up and down like juggling balls. Maybe I could sell them, too!*

"Poppa, how much money do the wood fishers get for the scraps of wood they pull from the Mississippi?" asked Fritz.

"What was that, Fritjof?" Poppa looked up.

"Wood fishers, Poppa. How much do they make each day?"

"Oh, I've heard about three dollars if they sell a whole cord of wood."

"A cord? That's a huge stack!" said Fritz.

Fritz stared at his plate. It did not seem like any of his ideas would add up to much.

The next morning Fritz woke with a new plan. He nudged Poppa. "I want to work, too, Poppa. I finished fifth grade last week. Could we ask Uncle Henning about a job for me on his stonecutting crew for the new bridge?"

Poppa sat on the edge of the bed. He sighed. "You're so young, Fritz, but I guess you're right. The boat trip from Sweden costs a lot. We'll go see Henning."

Fritz always liked going to his uncle's house. The walls were whitewashed bright and clean and hung with lots of shelves to show off all his rocks, shells, and fossils. Uncle Henning couldn't bear to leave his collections behind when he left Sweden, so he brought all he could with him. Fritz knew how much his uncle missed being a science teacher.

"*Halla*, Uncle Henning!" Fritz called as he bolted through the doorway over to the shelf where his favorite rock lay with its label: "tinguanite, Mt. Fulufjället, Dalarna, Sweden." Fritz rubbed the smooth rock with his thumb and examined the pale green areas blending into dark green with squiggly black lines, like a miniature map of a river running through a deep forest. It reminded him of the day Uncle Henning took everyone to see the three-hundred-foot waterfall at Mt. Fulufjället. It seemed like a long time ago, walking through reindeer moss to look for the glowing green rocks that could only be found in that part of Sweden.

Fritz heard Poppa discussing his plan with Henning. Did Henning think Fritz was strong enough to chisel the limestone? Could he work long hours every day? Agreeing to ask his boss, Henning said, "We need all the hands we can get if we're to meet Mr. Hill's fall deadline to cross the Mississippi River with his stone arch bridge. James J. Hill wants his railway to go all the way to the West Coast—what a dream. You know, some are calling it 'Hill's Folly'!"

The next day at the quarry, Fritz paced back and forth. He watched as his uncle talked with the boss. Finally, the boss nodded. The answer was "yes"!

Fritz became the youngest worker on the crew. He found the smallest wooden mallet, but it still seemed bulky. The chisel was much heavier than it looked. Uncle Henning helped him trim over ten inches off a leather apron so it wouldn't catch around his ankles. DAK, DAK, CLACK. Fritz put all his strength into his work. Hadn't he won the handstand contest?

Mr. Andrews, the boss, checked on Fritz every day, towering over him. Fritz felt the hulking man's eyes pierce through him. Fritz's hands shook so much that his mallet tumbled to the ground. He looked down at the blisters popping open on his hand and stopped to rub his sore arm. "Not making much progress today, are you, boy?" the boss snarled, lumbering off.

DAK, DAK, CLACK, CLATTER. Fritz tried to focus on the sounds of his labor.

One afternoon as Fritz chiseled, his mallet stopped in midair. There were marks already on the limestone—marks he hadn't made with his chisel. Fritz kneeled down, peering at the tiny lines. The three-inch oval reminded him of something that could swim, like a creature from the ocean they crossed to get to America. It had two quarter-moon shapes on it, like tiny eyes. "Uncle Henning, come look at this," Fritz called.

"Amazing, Fritjof! You found a fossil of a marine animal long extinct—a trilobite. I've been reading about this part of America. Millions of years ago it was under a tropical, shallow sea. As the sea dried up, the animal shells combined to make the limestone we're working on today. That's why the Mississippi River bed is made of limestone and why the waterfall is here, too. Let's show the crew."

The Pyramid

FROM THAT DAY ON, FRITZ'S CHISEL SEEMED TO work a little faster. DAK, DAK, CLACK, CLACK. Someone from the crew smiled at him whenever he looked up. One man with a huge mustache even called over, "You have a keen eye, boy. Not many workers would notice that tiny fossil."

Uncle Henning said, "I bet your poppa's adding garlic to your supper every night. You seem to be getting stronger and stronger. Did you know the workers who built the pyramids in Egypt ate garlic to make themselves strong? We learned from the Egyptians how to chisel the limestone and move the blocks into place with just men and horses. It took tens of thousands of Egyptians many years to build each pyramid. We have over six hundred men working on our bridge, and James J. Hill wants it finished before winter."

"Do you think we'll make it?" Fritz asked. "It's already July."

"Maybe, if we all keep working hard and there aren't any more accidents."

"Oh, yes, Uncle, I heard what happened to Mr. Donovan when that whiffletree bar snapped off the windlass. That bar knocked him right in the head!"

"*Ay*, Fritz, we were all hoping Joseph Schmidt would be the only casualty when his boat tipped into the icy waters last February. Now that's two workers who died building the new bridge."

"And the draft horse died too, Uncle. It was thrown into a ditch from all that spinning power." Fritz put his head down and picked up his mallet. He didn't want anyone to see his tears as he remembered their horse back in Sweden. *Nothing like that better happen to Dale,* he thought. *Momma liked that name for our horse because he was stocky like all the toy horses the carvers made from scraps of wood in Dalarna. Momma has over thirty Dala horses in her collection. She promised to give Dale lots of hugs.*

Using his sleeve to wipe his eyes, Fritz whacked extra hard at the limestone block. *I'm going to need more and more garlic. What does garlic even look like?* Fritz thought. *I better check the garden Poppa planted behind our house. With all that rich, black mud we brought up from the river bottom, the plants are growing by leaps and bounds.* DAK, DAK, CLACK. Fritz tapped a pyramid shape into the block to remind him to be strong like the Egyptian workers.

The Roman Arch

THE NEXT DAY AT THE QUARRY, FRITZ IMAGINED how the bridge would look when all the limestone blocks were in place. *Twenty-three arches! Phew, that's going to take a lot of work. Everyone says Mr. Hill wants it to look like a Roman viaduct that carried water all across Europe. How did the Romans build so many arches?*

When Momma told us tales of gods and goddesses, she always said the Romans were very smart, he thought. *My favorite bedtime story was about the twin sons of the god Mars. Just after they were born, an evil uncle placed them in a wooden trough and cast them into a raging river a lot like the Mississippi here. When they washed ashore, a wolf named Lupa found the babies and took them to a cave to care for them. They grew strong. One of them was named Romulus. He founded the city named Rome. I think something bad happened to the other boy, Remus, but Momma never told us about that. She just hugged us, tucked the fluffy quilts all around us, and said,* "god natt, sov gott"—*good night, sweet dreams.*

The boss's heavy footsteps interrupted Fritz's daydream. He quickly hunkered down to work. DAK, DAK, CLACK, CLANG.

"Hey, boy, look at that stone you're working on—it's a perfect wedge shape for one of the keystones. Don't damage it, now. We need strong blocks to set at the top of each arch to force the energy right, left, and down the piers to the ground. Can you handle that, Fritz? That's your name, Fritz, right?" He strolled away, not waiting for a reply.

Wow, the boss knows my name! Fritz said to himself. *I better not ruin this one. What'd he call it? A keystone?* Fritz tapped a Roman arch shape into the stone as he worked. DAK, DAK, CLACK, CLACK.

Fritz headed home that day, racing down all seventy-nine shaky steps to the flats. He noticed Poppa's work boots all covered with flour dust propped against the side of the house. "*Hej*, you beat me!" he said, bounding in the door. "Mmmmm . . . what smells so delicious?"

"I've fixed your favorite dinner—meatballs and gravy—just like Momma makes, but I put in extra amounts of one ingredient. Can you guess?"

"Garlic, Poppa?"

"Yes, my expert stonecutter. They're going to pay you $1.25 every day now, just like the rest of the crew. Before we know it, the Persson family will be together again."

Fritz beamed as he gobbled down his supper.

The Eagle Feather

UNCLE HENNING HOLLERED OUT TO FRITZ AS SOON as he appeared at work the next morning.

"C'mon, a few of us are rowing over to the island. There's work to be done on the limestone there," he said.

The crew headed down Second Street toward the boat landing. They passed Brown's Livery Stable and turned onto Main Street. Fritz paused at the Union Iron Works and leaned in the doorway. Sweat ran down his face as he watched the workers forge parts for the huge machines at the flour mills. He jumped backward when some of the hot iron bubbled and sputtered out of the cauldron. "I don't think I could work here all day," Fritz said out loud.

"Hey, Uncle Henning, look!

"I can tell Poppa I saw how they make parts for his flour-packing machines. Uncle Henning . . . Uncle

Henning . . ." Fritz turned around and looked up and down the bustling street.

They're way ahead of me now, he thought. *I better take a shortcut.* He barreled down the cliff to the river's edge.

"Whoa, hold on! You almost knocked me flat," said a girl on the muddy path.

"Sorry, I didn't see you all hunched over. What are you staring at on the ground?"

"I'm not sure that's any of your business, but . . . see these tracks? Four toes on the front prints, five claws on the back ones, and there's that swoosh from the tail dragging along."

"Yes—do you know what animal was here?" Fritz asked.

"Of course I do!" the girl said as she straightened up, her dark eyes flashing. "I follow porcupines all the time. I gather the quills they shake off."

"What for?" Fritz asked.

"You ask a lot of questions. Maybe I'll show you what I make sometime. Gaag—that's his Ojibwe name—headed into the river," she said as she got to the last print. "Yeah, there it is swimming over to the place the Dakota call Wanagi Wita or Spirit Island. There's usually lots of quills over there. I'm going to get my Grandpa Bottineau's old boat. Bye!"

As she darted away, Fritz noticed a colorful, long pouch bouncing up and down at her waist. He turned and saw the stonecutting crew down at the boat landing. *Lucky for me they're still loading up,* Fritz thought. He hurdled over the bushes and branches blocking his path and joined the crew, gasping for air.

"Fritz, where have you been? Watch out, the boss may be checking on us," Uncle Henning warned.

"I know, I know," Fritz muttered, as his chin touched his chest.

The crew found huge chunks of limestone on the craggy island to shape into blocks with their mallets and chisels. As Fritz swung the mallet with all his might, his muscles gave way and sweat and grit got in his eyes. He searched under the tall cedar trees for smaller fragments to work on. Hearing the "Break time!" call, he flopped down against a hollow log.

"Hey, wake up! What in the world do you think you're doing? You're squishing the porcupine quills," the girl cried out, standing over him with her arms akimbo. Fritz blinked his eyes, stood up, and backed out of her way. "It's you! Are you going to ask me all sorts of questions again?" she said as she picked up quills, placing them in her bright container.

"Well, . . . yes. If I help you find more quills, will you tell me what you do with them?"

"I do need a lot . . ." she said. "Okay, put them here in my parfleche."

"So that's what you call it. I like the pattern on it. How did it get that name?"

"*Parfleche* means 'deflect arrows' in French," she said. "It's made from stiff buffalo hides, the same way shields were made a long time ago. My Grandpa Pierre's mother, Mizhakwadookwe, or 'Clear Sky Woman,' made one just like it for him to keep his prized possessions safe. She was also called Margaret—that's my name, too."

"Hello, Margaret. My name's Fritz. You know, my grandpa's name is Per. He lives in Sweden. 'Per' and 'Pierre,' they sound alike."

"Yeah—Pierre's a French name. My grandpa knows seven languages. He was a frontier guide and a fur trader. Some people still call him 'Walking Peace Pipe' because he helped people understand each other. Métis people could do that, because we're related to French, Ojibwe, and Dakota people."

"I know about the French, but who are the others?" Fritz asked.

"They lived here before the Americans came, and they still do. This part of Minnesota is Dakota land, and the northern part is Ojibwe. I can speak French, Ojibwe, and some Dakota."

"I speak Swedish, and I've learned lots of English. I've wondered about who lived here before."

Margaret and Fritz circled about, filling up the parfleche. "Come over here, there are more quills by this rocky den," said Fritz. "Ouch, these quills are sharp!"

"Watch out for those barbs. Now, all I need are some sumac berries."

"What are they for?" Fritz asked.

Margaret sighed. "I use the berries to dye some of the quills bright red. Then I flatten the quills and soak them, so I can string them into bracelets or sew them onto birch bark. See these dangles on my parfleche? They were made by wrapping dyed quills around pieces of hide."

"Would you show me how to make a parfleche? I have something I want to keep safe," said Fritz.

"Well, . . . maybe someday."

* * *

While Fritz looked for more quills for his new friend, he spotted a long brown and white feather. "Look, Margaret, I suppose you know which bird this came from?" he said.

"It's an eagle feather! Can I hold it? Don't drop it, now. You're very lucky to have found it. Wambdi, the eagle, is one of my favorite relatives. *Mitakuyapi,* that means 'all living things together, all my relations' in Dakota."

"Oh, yes, I like them, too. Sometimes I spread out flat on my back and watch the eagles swoop and dive. They're powerful, and those talons look really sharp."

"My grandpa told me a story about eagles that happened here over two hundred winter counts ago," said Margaret. "A priest named Louis Hennepin was brought to the waterfall by the buffalo hunters. All through their spring travels there was little to eat, but the eagles often dropped pieces of fish from their beaks as they soared high in the sky. Father Hennepin was grateful that the eagles went fishing for him! He named the waterfall St. Anthony Falls, after the saint who protects travelers."

"*Ay,* he should have named it Eagle Falls! Is that why we have Hennepin Island and Hennepin Avenue with that first bridge? Are they all named after him?"

"Yes, and now you do need your own parfleche to keep your eagle feather safe. Maybe you'll do a brave deed someday. Then you can wear the feather for all to see."

"Oh, and I want to keep the money I make every day in it, too. My poppa and I are saving to bring my momma and sisters here from Sweden."

"Your mother doesn't live here with you?" Margaret asked, her eyes wide.

Fritz answered in a soft voice, "Not yet. My poppa and I have been here for almost a whole year."

The silence between them lasted a few minutes, but then Fritz snapped to when he heard the DAK, DAK, CLANG, CLATTER of chisels hitting stone. "Oh, Margaret, I have to go. I bet our work break is long over."

He raced away, waving over his shoulder to his new friend. "Bye!"

As Fritz drew close to the work site, he heard a deep voice shouting at the crew, "Fan out now, get some real work done." Mr. Andrews was here!

Fritz skidded to a stop and tried to hide, but the boss had seen him. "And you, boy, you just lost a day's pay," he yelled. "You haven't worked the whole time I've been here. I ought to fire you!" With that, the boss leapt into his boat and headed back to shore.

Fritz's knees buckled, and he sank to the ground. "How can I tell Poppa I didn't earn any money today?"

The crew called out to him, "Hey, Fritz, we've worked hard on this solid wedge for another keystone. You can finish it off."

Fritz lifted his mallet—it seemed heavier than ever before. DAK . . . CLANG . . .

The afternoon wore on. Finally, it was time to load up the rowboat. *At least this keystone's ready for one more arch on the bridge,* Fritz thought as he looked it over. Remembering Margaret's story, he took time to tap an eagle feather into the keystone. DAK, DAK, CLACK, CLACK, CLANG.

The North Star

THE NEXT DAY AT THE QUARRY, THE BOSS KEPT A watchful eye on the men. Fritz swung his mallet with all his might and never took a break. *Phew!* he thought. *I made it through without the boss bellowing at me about what happened at Spirit Island. And I can't wait to tell Poppa the big news the boss just announced.*

"Poppa, guess what?" Fritz said that evening. "I'm going to be in a photograph! Mr. Jacoby is coming tomorrow to take the stonecutter crew's picture for Mr. Hill."

"Oh, Fritz, that will be something to write to Momma about! See, I told you not to fret when you lost one day's pay. Good things always follow bad. Let's wash your overalls tonight."

"I wish my straw hat didn't have that big hole in it," Fritz said. "Momma would know how to fix it."

"Fritz, that photographer is the best in town—a real artist. A few years back, he picked out a negative of a photo of the old Washburn 'A' Mill and painted and scratched on it until it actually looked like a picture of the mill as it exploded that spring night in '78. What a disaster! People said everything went flying five hundred feet in the air. From miles away they thought it was an earthquake. Eighteen people died. You know my friend Henry at the mill? He's always talking about how much he misses August and Ole, who were killed instantly." Poppa's voice dropped. "I'm glad we weren't here then." He cleared his throat. "Anyway, I'm sure Mr. Jacoby will do a good job on your crew photo for Mr. Hill."

Fritz popped out of bed the next morning. He jabbed his arms into the sleeves of his best shirt and pulled on his clean overalls. As he grabbed his hat and bolted out the door, a big smile washed over his face. "Good as new," Fritz thought as he punched the straw bowler down over his forehead. "I have the best poppa!"

Mr. Jacoby was already setting his big box camera on top of the tripod when Fritz arrived. "Let's get you all over here by the flatbed cart before you get too grimy and covered with dust. Bring your mallets and chisels," he called out. "Okay, tall guys in the back, and you, boy, sit right here in the middle."

Even the boss sat down off to the side, looking important in his black suit and tie. *I'm glad he didn't sit next to me*, thought Fritz.

"Okay, gentlemen, eyes here. Look strong. Hold it now," Mr. Jacoby said.

Fritz squirmed and shifted his legs, but held his

mallet high. "I can't wait to see the photograph," he said to Uncle Henning.

Later that day, Fritz wished he didn't have his best shirt and clean overalls on. They were caked with grit, grime, and sweat. The sun's blistering rays bounced off the limestone right into his eyes. Everyone on the crew was groaning loudly. The boss decided to be generous for a change. "Let's quit early today. Go cool off by the river," he called.

"Yee-hee! What a surprise!" Fritz ran back home lickety-split, popping into the shade here and there to catch his breath. He changed into his short pants and set out to look for his friends. "*Hej*, Sven, Nils, Lise— where are you?" No one was out on the flats.

Fritz went to the end of one of the platforms jutting into the river and dangled his feet in the water. "Ahhh," he sighed to himself. "I guess it's even too hot for the wood fishers to be working today." He looked upstream and saw an old rowboat riding the current toward him. "Whoa, watch out! You're gonna crash into the platform!" he yelled. The rower veered off and circled around just in time. Fritz stared. It was Margaret in her grandpa's boat.

"*Boozhoo*, Fritz. It seemed like a good day to get on the water, but I can hardly keep up with the Mississippi today," she said.

"Yeah, I wanted to go swimming, but the river's really churning and the logs are bouncing all over the place. All that sawdust and flour dust makes for a gooey mess. And it stinks," he said.

"I know. Wanna go over to Lake Calhoun?" Margaret asked. "Grandpa Bottineau showed me a trail to this big, clear lake. Have you ever been?"

"No—*Nu kor vi*: let's go!" said Fritz.

Margaret tied up her boat. They scrambled up the steps from the flats to Cedar Avenue and headed off to hike the trail.

"See," Margaret said, pointing at the ground. "If you look closely, sometimes you can make out three grooves on the path. They're from the *travois*, the tipi poles that the Dakota fastened to a horse to take their canvas covers, food, and supplies up north when they went to gather wild rice. They left right after they harvested their corn, beans, and squash at Lake Calhoun. I wonder what it would be like to move around so much."

"At least they had their whole family with them," said Fritz.

"Let's hurry," Margaret said. "I'm sweating up a storm."

"I see the lake up ahead. What blue, blue waters. Whoopee!" Fritz yelled.

They dove in and splashed and swam in the lake. The water was refreshingly cool.

"I sure like Lake Calhoun!" Fritz said, treading water.

"My grandpa calls it by its Dakota name, 'Mdoza,' Lake of Loons. Have you ever seen a loon?"

"What does it look like?" asked Fritz as he flipped onto his back.

"Its black head shimmers bright green in the sunshine, and it has white stripes around its neck—like it's wearing a fancy necklace. It has red eyes and its belly is solid white, but all along the black feathered back there are white dots, like stars. I love to see the babies riding on their mother's back. I hope you hear their call sometime. It sounds kind of eerie. Makes you want to call back."

"That seems a lot like the *lom* bird we have in Sweden, but ours has a shiny red throat. Does it look clumsy when it tries to walk on land?" Fritz asked.

"Yes, yes it does! Grandpa Bottineau says it's because its little legs are set far back on its body, so it can swim fast. I'd like to see one with a red throat," said Margaret.

"Race you back to shore!" Fritz said, and then he dove deep, holding his breath. When Margaret saw him pop up for air out ahead of her, she thrashed her arms with all her might.

"Tie!" they both called out with grins on their faces as they stood up on the sandy beach.

"That felt so good. What a wonderful spot to cool off," said Fritz.

"We better head back," said Margaret. "Come this way. I know a shortcut."

She picked up the pace until Fritz asked her to slow down a bit.

"Okay, let's go in here. I want to show you something," said Margaret. Fritz looked past the creaky wooden gate Margaret had stopped at. "A cemetery? Do you think we should?"

"Sure, we can say haŋ to Nahhenowenahwiŋ—

'Spirit of the Moon.' Her band lived near Lake Calhoun. In fact, her father was a Dakota chief, 'Man Who Flies.' My grandpa told me she was strong and smart. See, here it says 'Mary Prescott' on her stone. She married Philander Prescott when he came from Fort Snelling to Lake Calhoun and showed some Dakota men who were taking up farming how to use a plow. He knew many languages, just like my grandpa. Here's his gravestone and their son's, too: Lorenzo Taliferro Prescott. He was a soldier in the Civil War."

"I don't know too much about that war, but I sure know all about plowing," said Fritz. "I helped my poppa plow the fields back home in Sweden. Sometimes we could hardly budge that old rickety plow through the soil with all the rocks and plants and roots in the way."

Fritz glanced over at the names on some of the other headstones. His eye caught the word *miller*. "Oh, it's August Smith, and there's Ole Schei. My poppa was just telling me how they were killed instantly in that huge explosion that leveled some flour mills a few years ago."

"I was only five, but I'll never forget what happened that night," said Margaret. "Let's sit down and I'll tell you about it. Our family had just finished supper when we heard a huge BOOM! Our whole house shook. Dishes crashed to the floor. My mother screamed, 'It's the end of the world! It's the end of the world!' My father bolted out the door, so my mother grabbed my hand and we ran after him." Margaret shifted in the grass and when on. "Everyone rushed down to the riverbank. Across the river, flames were shooting hundreds of feet in the air. We heard more booms, and the fire just kept spreading. My mother squeezed me tight and sobbed.

"All of a sudden, our neighbor, Mr. Peasely, clutched his heart, fell to his knees, and made this awful wailing sound. He took off toward the bridge screaming that he had to help rescue the millers. You see, everyone knew that it should have been Mr. Peasely in that inferno because he usually worked the night shift. But another miller had asked him to switch to the day shift in order to organize a baseball league. Mr. Peasely's life had been spared that night."

Fritz's eyes grew wide and his mouth dropped open. Even though five years had passed, Margaret still seemed frantic at the memory. Fritz frowned and lowered his head. "That must have been terrible for you and your family to witness," he whispered.

Margaret looked down, her eyes closed tight. Tears trickled down her cheeks. She got to her feet and started to run through the cemetery.

Fritz tried to catch up. "Margaret, look up—stop!" he yelled.

Just as Margaret raised her blurry eyes off the ground, she plowed headfirst into one of the tall weeping-angel monuments. Fritz watched in horror as her whole body bounced off the stone figure and hurled backward. Margaret landed spread-eagle in the dirt.

"Oh, no!" Fritz cried. He knelt down and cradled her head in his lap, lightly tapping her cheeks. "Margaret, say something. Are you okay? Say something, please!"

"Eee, eee—ow," Margaret whimpered.

Fritz let out a huge sigh.

"Wha . . . what happened?" she whispered.

Fritz felt a bump popping up on Margaret's forehead. "You better rest awhile. Don't try to talk," he said.

He propped Margaret against a nearby oak tree. She snuggled into the mossy hollow of the gnarly trunk. "Stay still, now," he said.

As he sat down next to Margaret, his hand hit something sharp in the moss. He dug around the squared-off edge until he could pull it out of the hollow.

"What's this? Look, Margaret, look. It's like some secret tin box." Fritz held the box in his hand. "A little rusty here and there. I wonder what it's doing here? What do you think's inside?"

Margaret just groaned and shifted onto her side.

Fritz pried open the box. Inside was a cloth with letters carefully stitched on it:

TOUSSAINT

"What does that mean?" Fritz wondered aloud. Then he noticed a curl of dark hair attached to the cloth with a red and blue striped ribbon. Under the cloth there was a tiny toy drum, a prancing horse carved out of wood, a railroad boxcar, and a picture of a man on horseback. At the bottom of the picture was an inscription:

GENERAL TOUSSAINT L'OUVERTURE—GOVERNOR OF HAITI

"Wow, a general! Look at his silver sword and fancy

hat. Who could have left all this here? I wish you could take a look, Margaret."

Fritz stood up, stretched his legs and walked around the tree. "*Hej*, there's that same name on this headstone: Toussaint L'Ouverture Grey, April 11, 1859–June 28, 1868. It can't be the same man in that picture. This person only lived to be nine years old."

"Eee, eee—*ow!*" Margaret groaned louder this time and inched her back up the bark of the tree.

Fritz rushed to her side. "Careful. You have quite a bump here. Do you feel dizzy?"

"No, no, I'm feeling better now," Margaret said as she tapped her forehead. Then her hand bumped the tiny drum. "What's all this? Are they toys?"

"I don't know. They were here in this old tin box, half buried inside the tree trunk. What do you make of them?" Fritz said.

"Toussaint." Margaret looked at the cloth. "That's a French name."

"And the same name is over there on that gravestone," Fritz said. "He was just nine when he died."

"Oh, these must be his toys, then. Do you think his mother and father left them here? I like this perky horse with the long wavy tail," said Margaret.

"That's my favorite, too. It's a lot fancier than our Dalarna wooden horses that people carve in Sweden. Sometime I'll show you the one I brought with me to remind me of Dale, our horse back home."

"You had a horse?" asked Margaret.

"Yes, he worked hard on our farm. I took real good care of him."

Margaret rose to her knees. "We better put this all back in the hollow and get on our way. It's starting to get dark."

"Yeah, it's cooling off finally. I hope I get home before Poppa does," said Fritz.

They passed through the wooden gate of the cemetery and made their way back onto the Lake Calhoun trail. All the while, Fritz kept thinking about the boy named Toussaint.

"*Hej*, do you know anything about that place called Haiti that was on the picture in the tin box?" he asked.

"Nope." Margaret stumbled a bit on the trail.

"I better walk in front of you," said Fritz. "Say, why did you take off running back in the cemetery, anyway?"

Margaret looked away and spoke softly. "Both of my friend's brothers died in the explosion. And he almost did, too. He liked to go with them to the mill, and usually his mother said okay. But she wouldn't let him go along that night. It was as if she knew, like she had a premonition or something. I was remembering how sad we were all summer long. I guess I needed to get away from those gravestones."

Fritz took her hand and squeezed it tight. He stood strong and let Margaret lean on his shoulder. "Let's get you back to your house now."

The next few days at the quarry, Fritz had to trudge through drifts of sludge in his old work boots. "Uncle Henning, do you think it will ever stop raining? I can hardly squish through this muck."

"Yeah, I wish Mr. Hill would give us those tall rubber boots like the ones he issued the crew down at the bridge site," said Uncle Henning. "Watch out now, those mounds of stone dust can get pretty slick in this weather."

"Hey, boy! Fritz! Get over here pronto!" the boss called out.

"Uh-oh. I wonder what he wants." Fritz picked up one boot covered with goo and then the other and tried to build up speed. By the time he approached the boss, he was running pretty fast. WHOOSH, SPLAT! Fritz hit a wet glob and landed on his back. His arms and legs thrashed in the air.

The boss let out a big belly laugh. "You look like a pig wallowing in the mud. C'mon now, boy. I need you to run an errand," he said.

Fritz gulped and struggled to his feet. He was glad to see that the boss was grinning.

"I think our crew photo is ready. Run over to Jacoby's Gallery on Nicollet and bring it back to me. Mr. Hill is anxious to gather all the crews' photographs," he said.

"Yes, sir! I'll do my best."

Fritz stomped his boots every step of the way across the suspension bridge and rubbed at the dirt on his cheeks. "Maybe the wind will dry off these muddy overalls before I reach Bridge Square," he said out loud.

There sure are a lot of people out and about on Nicollet Avenue, Fritz thought as he looked up and down the street. *What a big hotel, and there's City Hall. Look what's in the windows of that store called Ingram-Olson: fancy dresses, bonnets, and aprons. Momma would love to shop there! What do all these signs say? "Organs, Pianos," "Tailors," "Spring Beds."*

The next sign had a picture of a big camera on it. "Ah, here it is. 252 Nicollet, Wm. Jacoby's Gallery and Photo Studio," he read aloud. Fritz took a big breath as he stepped through the doorway.

He heard the man behind the counter say, "Mrs. Grey, I've got your granddaughter's photo right here. Emma sure is a beautiful baby." A tall lady wearing a striped cotton dress with a white collar and puffy sleeves took it from him and gazed down at the photo, her bluish-gray eyes twinkling.

"Oh, yes, she is. Emma reminds me of my own babies back in the day, especially Toussaint. I'll never forget crooning their favorite lullabies with the plaintive tones of St. Anthony Falls in the background as I'd rock them to sleep in the quiet twilight hours. You know, Mr. Jacoby, the falls don't sound like music anymore. All those dikes and dams and aprons forcing the mighty Mississippi into the turbines for power. It's a shame. *Tsk, tsk.*"

Fritz watched as she pulled out a hanky and dabbed at tears trickling down her cheeks. "Oh, I am so saddened when I think of my little Toussaint, my first baby born in St. Anthony all those years ago. I wonder what he would be like now. Would he have a sweet baby girl like Emma here?" she said.

"He certainly died way too young, Mrs. Grey," said Mr. Jacoby.

Fritz stood frozen in the doorway. *Could it be?* he thought. *She did say "Toussaint"—I'm sure of it. Is she the mother of the boy whose grave Margaret and I saw in the cemetery? Did she place that tin box in the hollow of the tree?*

Mr. Jacoby looked over at Fritz. "Well, come in, boy, but first try and shuffle some of that mud off your boots at the mat. What can I do for you?"

"Boss sent me to pick up the stonecutter's crew photo, sir. He needs to get it to Mr. Hill right away," Fritz said.

"Yes, it's ready. We sure don't want to keep James J. Hill waiting! Excuse me a minute, Mrs. Grey," said Mr. Jacoby.

Mrs. Grey smiled at Fritz. "Is something wrong?" she asked. "You look like you've seen a ghost."

"Ah . . . ah . . . I . . . I . . ." Fritz muttered.

"Do you have something to say? You can talk to me. Maybe I can help," said Mrs. Grey.

"Well, . . . I . . . I was wondering. You see, me and my friend were at this cemetery on the way home from Lake Calhoun just the other day and . . . and . . . my friend fell, so we rested by this big oak tree and . . . and . . . we found a tin box and . . . and . . . we . . . we opened it," said Fritz.

"Oh, I see." Mrs. Grey put her hand up to her mouth. "I hope you were careful. All the things in that box are very special to me. They have helped me keep my son Toussaint's memory alive over all these years."

"Yes, yes, we were very gentle with everything. We tucked the tin box back into its mossy spot. Could . . .

could . . . I ask you about the picture of that strong man on horseback with the grand feather on his hat? Why was it in the box with the toys?" said Fritz.

"Well, yes you may ask. I can tell you all about that brave leader. What is your name, boy?" Mrs. Grey asked.

"My name is Fritz—Fritz Persson, ma'am."

"So, Fritz, my husband, Ralph, and I named our boy 'Toussaint' in honor of General Toussaint L'Ouverture, the governor of Haiti," said Mrs. Grey. "He led a revolt against the French rulers in that small island country and freed all the slaves there. We hoped our Toussaint would grow up to be strong like him. Alas, it was not meant to be—his little heart gave way." Mrs. Grey moved closer and looked into the boy's eyes. "How old are you, Fritz?"

"Ten years old, ma'am. I'll be eleven soon. I start sixth grade next month."

"I thought so," said Mrs. Grey. "Toussaint was almost your age when he died." She took a deep breath. "Would you like to hear a story from the past, Fritz? You see, I helped to free a slave right here in Minnesota. Her name was Eliza . . . Eliza Winston."

"Oh, yes, I would like that very much," said Fritz, forgetting all about his errand.

"Do you have any idea what it meant to be a slave, Fritz?"

"No, not really. My teacher talked some about the Civil War last year, but she said we'd learn more about it this year," said Fritz.

"Oh, good. Maybe you can share Eliza's story with

your class, then. Let's sit down over there on that tufted bench. Mr. Jacoby, can you hear me back there?" she called out.

"What is it, Mrs. Grey?"

"You take your time, now. That boy's boss will get his photograph soon enough. Fritz and I are getting to know each other here," she said.

Mr. Jacoby looked out from behind the velvet curtain and watched the twosome settle in on his bench. He noticed Fritz look up at Mrs. Grey with soft blue eyes and a contented smile. "Sure thing," he called back to her.

"Ah, where do I begin?" Mrs. Grey sighed. "You see, Fritz, Ralph and I were territorial pioneers. Ralph left our home in Pennsylvania and started up his barbershop in St. Anthony. Soon, our first son, William, and I followed him. Minnesota wasn't even an official state yet. I sorely missed my family back east. My father owned thirteen railroad freight cars, a barbershop, and an office building called Centre Hall. Oh my, I'm going back in time here. My brother's photography studio on the top floor of that building looked just like Mr. Jacoby's here." Mrs. Grey cleared her throat. "My father had been born a slave but was given his freedom when he was sixteen. Our family always helped slaves who came north seeking to be free. We would hide them in our home or the office building or smuggle them further north in the freight cars. Everyone called that the 'Underground Railroad,' but it wasn't anything like the comfortable train trip William and I took to Minnesota.

"Anyway, one hot summer, Eliza Winston was brought to St. Anthony from Mississippi by Colonel Richard Christmas, who had owned her for seven years. The Christmas family came here to escape the unbearable heat down south and enjoy St. Anthony Falls and the Chalybeate Mineral Springs. Have you ever taken a ride on the flatboats into the tunnels at the springs, Fritz?"

"Oh, no. My poppa and I work almost every day," said Fritz.

"Well, I hope you get a chance to take a boat ride someday.

"So, Eliza stayed with the Christmas family at the Winslow House near where my Ralph had his barbershop. It wasn't long before she was able to get word to me that she needed help. She wanted to be free. You see, slavery isn't allowed in Minnesota and other Northern states. I knew Judge Vanderburgh, who came to Minnesota from New York, didn't believe people should be owned like property. He ordered the sheriff to bring Eliza to his court. But Colonel Christmas had already left the Winslow House and had taken Eliza out to a cottage on Lake Harriet. So, a posse was formed— about thirty men with guns—to bring her back."

Fritz sat up straight. "They all had guns? Rifles even?" he said.

"Yes. I knew Eliza would be terrified of all the men and the horses and wagons and guns, so I talked to my neighbor, Mrs. Bates, and we decided to accompany the posse. When Mrs. Christmas heard us all coming, she ordered Eliza to hide out in back in the hazel

bushes. But, as soon as Eliza saw me and Mrs. Bates, she ran down the path toward us. Thank goodness there was no trouble. At least, not at the time!"

"Phew, I'm glad no one was hurt," said Fritz.

"Well, just you wait. Let me tell you. Even though the hot air was heavy with moisture and the mosquitoes were buzzing all around us, Mrs. Bates, Eliza, and I huddled close down in the back of the wagon. The posse had their guns ready the whole ride back to the courthouse on Fourth Street. Everyone at the yellow-brick doorway greeted us with cheers, but as we made our way upstairs to the packed courtroom, we heard jeers and angry protests from other folks. Judge Vanderburgh quickly declared Eliza 'free to go where and with whom she pleased.' That set off some noisy speeches! One pastor jumped up and accused the judge of making 'an unrighteous decision.' The people who wanted Southern slave owners to feel welcome in Minnesota and spend their money here yelled and stomped their feet.

"Oh, Fritz, I saw a lot of frightened faces about then. I was so relieved when Mr. Babbitt whisked Eliza away. Since he was part of the Underground Railroad, I knew he'd keep her safe. Too bad Eliza's story didn't end there.

"It started to rain hard that night, and by midnight it was blowing up into quite a storm. That didn't stop the howling mob of ruffians who came to our house searching for Eliza. They busted down our door and ransacked our shelves and cabinets, turning everything upside down. Little William wrapped his arms around my waist and buried his face in the folds of my nightdress. And, of course, baby Toussaint howled in my arms. I was so proud of my Ralph. He stood firm in front of us and yelled, 'Eliza Winston is not here! Get out of our home, now!'

"Later, we heard the same thing happened at Mr. Babbitt's house. Led by the owner of the Winslow House, Mr. McLean, the mob surrounded the Babbitt home from midnight to morning. They threw sticks and rocks and chanted, 'We want that slave!' Finally, when Mr. Babbitt screamed out, 'You cannot have her!' they used fence posts to batter down the solid walnut front door. That's when shots rang out and the mob backed away. Mrs. Babbitt, seven months pregnant, was able to sneak out their back door and run for help. When the sheriff arrived, he forced the mob to disperse. They kept shouting threats over their shoulders as they left."

"What happened to Eliza?" asked Fritz. "Was she safe? Did she get away?"

"Yes, I'm happy to say the Underground Railroad worked again. Eliza even came back in the fall and gave a speech at our Anti-Slavery Society meeting. But then she moved on. People still walked our streets with guns at the ready. There was such debate about this national crime of slavery in America. Of course, not long after that the Civil War began. Minnesota was one of the first states to send troops to preserve the Union and ban slavery everywhere."

Mrs. Grey turned her head and pointed to a painting on the wall. "Look at this glass painting Mr. Jacoby framed. See, Fritz. It has our state seal and motto on it, 'L'Etoile du Nord.' That's French for 'The North Star.'"

"Oh, just like Toussaint's name and Margaret's grandpa, Pierre Bottineau's name," said Fritz.

"Do you know Mr. Bottineau, Fritz? He is a most generous man," said Mrs. Grey. "He donated land for the mission church in St. Anthony, and he owns land west of here, too, so lots of people are settling out there now. I actually own some land near his in the black oaks savanna."

"No, I've never met Mr. Bottineau, but Margaret talks about him all the time. She's learned a lot from him. She even gets to use his old boat!" said Fritz.

"I'll never forget your story," he continued. "Thank you for telling it to me. You were so brave to help Eliza." Fritz inched closer to Mrs. Grey. "You make me think of my grandma back home in Sweden. Do you think I could call you 'Mormor'?"

"That would be just fine," said Mrs. Grey. She drew Fritz in close and gave him a warm hug.

Mr. Jacoby came out from the back room. "Boy, you'd better hurry along now and get this photo to your boss," he said, handing Fritz a flat box.

"Oh, let's see your picture, Fritz," said Mrs. Grey. "Where are you?"

Fritz opened the box and smiled. He pointed to the center of the photo.

Mrs. Grey smiled. "You look very industrious, Fritz," she said. "I bet you are a good worker."

"Thank you, Mormor. *Tusen tack*. I best be on my way. Thanks, Mr. Jacoby. Good-bye!"

Fritz ran all the way down Nicollet Avenue and across the Hennepin Bridge. "I can't wait to tell Poppa all about Mrs. Grey and Eliza and my photo. I'm so glad that Poppa picked Minnesota. The next time I get to work on a keystone for Mr. Hill's bridge, I'm going to chisel a star on it—the North Star!"

The Wheat Stalk

ONE HOT DAY IN LATE AUGUST, THE BOSS ARRIVED early at the quarry. He paced among the limestone blocks. "We need just one more keystone for the twenty-third arch. James J. Hill ordered all the stones to be in place at the bridge site. He'll fire me if we miss his September deadline," he said.

The crew murmured to each other with blank looks on their faces. They knew there weren't any more strong wedge-shaped blocks. They would have to go all the way to Mankato to search the quarry there. That would take days! Suddenly Uncle Henning took off carrying his tools in the direction of the Washburn "A" Mill, where Poppa worked. Fritz sped after him.

"Your poppa told me about a huge pile of limestone blocks left over when the mill was rebuilt after that terrible explosion. Let's go check."

Fritz and his uncle climbed and crawled, examining the blocks. Uncle Henning often stopped to chisel.

DAK, CLANG, CLATTER. Each block cracked or split into pieces.

Poppa was finished packing flour for the day, so he came out to see what was going on. "I hope your boss doesn't get fired. He's gruff, but fair," Poppa said when he heard about the hunt for the last keystone.

Just then Fritz's ears perked up to the "oom pah, oom pah" sounds of a tuba and the "boom, boom" of a big bass drum. "Oh, Poppa, Uncle Henning, some of the millers are practicing again for the big parade next week. Did you hear President Arthur and General Grant are coming? I can't wait! Can we go watch? Sven told me he would be there. His dad plays the trombone."

When they got to the practice area, the first thing they saw was a huge banner some of the millers were painting for the parade. In big letters it spelled out, GIVE US THE WHEAT AND WE WILL FEED THE WORLD.

"Wow, I'll have to tell Momma about that in my next letter. Feed the whole world. That is a tall order!" Fritz said.

Then he saw Sven sitting on a limestone block they always shared when they came to listen to the musicians practice. Fritz had even chiseled a wheat stalk on it one day as they watched all the box cars coming in from the Red River Valley filled with hard, red spring wheat. As Fritz got closer, he looked at their block in a new way.

"Uncle Henning, see what Sven's sitting on? It's a perfect wedge for a keystone!"

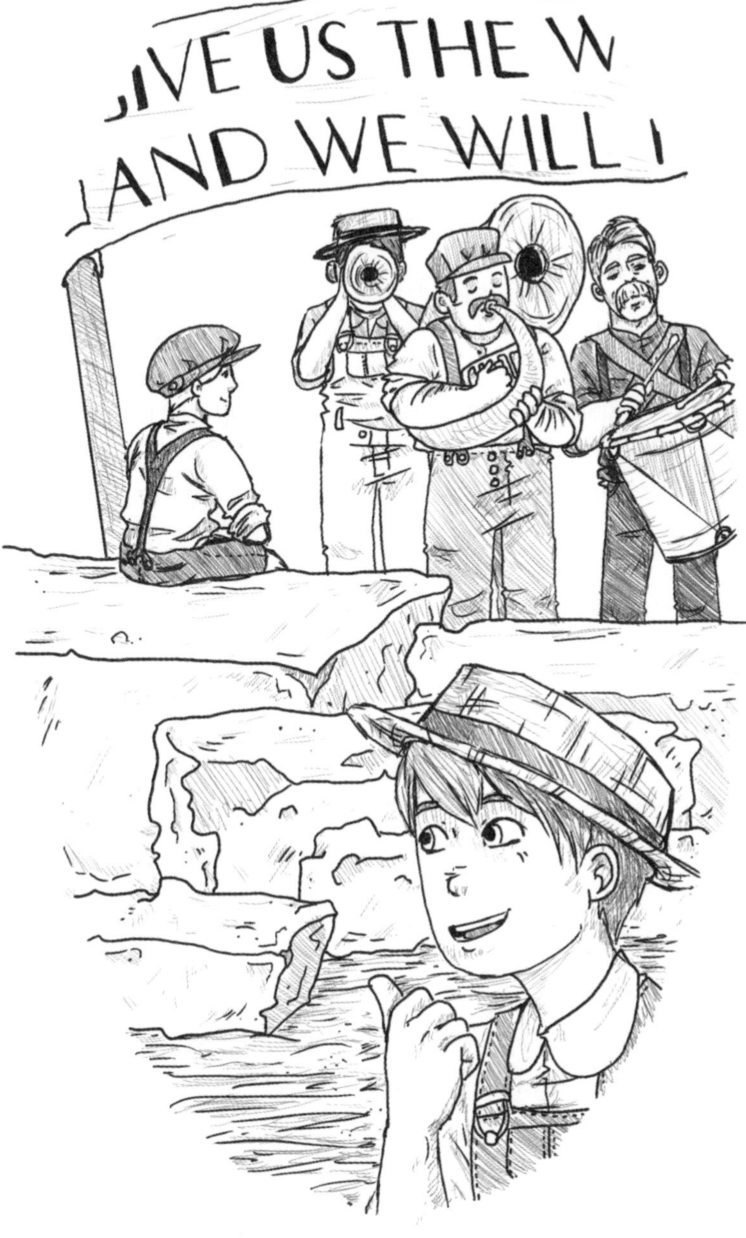
IVE US THE W
AND WE WILL

"I think you're right, Fritz. You have a keen eye, indeed! Go tell the boss."

Fritz raced back to the quarry. The boss was glad to go with him to the mill. "You and Henning came through just in time! There'll be a bonus for such top-notch workers," he said.

Fritz grinned at Poppa. He knew what he would do with his bonus.

The stonecutting crew started to move the limestone blocks down to the bridge site so they could be wedged into place. Fritz thought it was scary to see the keystones dropped at the top of each arch. He even heard that one more worker died when the centering frame underneath one arch collapsed, toppling the wooden timbers down on top of him. "I guess it's good that sixth grade at Adams School starts next week. Only a few more days to work," he said softly.

One day, Margaret came by to watch the construction. She had helped Fritz make his own parfleche, so she was happy to hear he had some bonus money to put in it. "You were clever to find that last keystone so your boss could meet his deadline. If you want, I can take your suspenders home and quill a design on them so you can slide your eagle feather through for all to see."

Fritz took in a big breath and smiled. "Thank you, Margaret, I would like that. I worked hard all summer with the crew. Poppa says it won't be long now before Momma and my sisters leave Sweden to come to America."

The Key

ONE FRIGID NOVEMBER NIGHT, FRITZ WRAPPED himself in all the threadbare quilts he could find and shuffled across the wooden floor, peering out each frosted windowpane of their house.

Poppa laughed. "You look like a caterpillar in its cocoon."

"Oh, Poppa, do you think this snowstorm will slow down Momma's train? She and Hannah and Inge have to come tomorrow."

"We'll go straight to the depot first thing. All we can do is wait and see."

The next morning Fritz raced ahead of Poppa, leaping over all the snowdrifts. "Now you look like a jackrabbit!" Poppa laughed again, just as he had so often back in Sweden.

At the depot Fritz counted five trains with lots of weary passengers getting off. But they had come in from the south. No trains from the east were getting through.

"Come, Fritz, we better head on home. The stationmaster says no other trains are expected today."

Fritz and Poppa trudged back along Washington Avenue. Neither liked the thought of another night alone in their little house. The new tall mast of eight arc lights back in Bridge Square sent its shadow way out ahead of them. Usually Fritz jumped, twisted, and waved his arms in order to make funny shadow shapes from the bright light of the "man-made moon." His favorite was to flip his legs up, walk on his hands, and yell "hee-haw, hee-haw." Poppa always laughed a full belly laugh over that one. Sometimes Sven and Nils came along and they played shadow tag. But not tonight. Tonight, Fritz and Poppa just plodded through the snow. When they reached the steep steps down to the flats, they heard a long "choo, choo" whistle and loud rumblings on the tracks.

"Could it be, Poppa? Maybe? We have to go back!"

Fritz ran faster than he ever had. From afar he saw porters unloading luggage. They handed off a brightly colored wooden trunk decorated with flowers and spirals. Around the lock was painted a plump red heart with a swirly capital "P."

"It's Momma's trunk! Hurry, Poppa. I think I see them."

Fritz crashed into Momma's arms, squeezing her tight. The five Perssons smothered each other with hugs and kisses. Everyone talked at once. Little Inge shrieked about the steam engine pushing through the snowdrifts. Hannah couldn't stop talking about the tall buildings and the new Brooklyn Bridge they saw in New York City. Momma kept saying, "Fritjof, Fritjof, my little Fritz. You have grown so."

Poppa fetched a wagon. "Let's go home," he said to his family.

The shanty house glowed with warmth and laughter. The squashed tin cans Poppa used to block every hole between the boards of the house glistened and seemed to say, "Välkommen." Hannah and Inge twirled around their new home, checking out each nook and cranny. Momma looked out each window. "Oh, Per," she said to Poppa, "I see a lone guardian spirit tree out there just like the *vardtrad* we left behind in our courtyard in Sweden. That's a good sign for our family's future here in Minnesota." Momma gave Poppa another big kiss. Even though all were exhausted, no one could sleep.

"Open the trunk, Momma, *snälla,* please!" Fritz said. "What did you bring from Sweden?"

"I do have something I think you need, Fritz," Momma said. "Where is my key? I had it in my cape pocket. Maybe here in my bag. No? Well, maybe in my sweater pocket? Oh, I hope it's not lost. Your grandpa forged it in his blacksmith shop."

Everyone searched. Fritz even stepped outside to check. There in the snow piling up on the doorstep lay the familiar heart-shaped key with a capital "P." Fritz gulped as he saw it again after all these months. He remembered it hanging in the parlor next to the family portrait. "*Ay*, I found it!" he said, bursting through the door.

"Oh, Fritjof, you are so clever." Momma turned the

key in the lock, lifted the lid of the trunk, and pulled out a lush, fluffy quilt covered with embroidered hearts and flowers. "No more threadbare quilts for you!"

Fritz gave Momma another hug. "*Tack såmycket*— thank you so much," he said. "And I have something for you." He went to the shelf by his bed to get the parfleche. "My friend Margaret helped me make this to keep prized possessions safe. Let's keep your key in it."

The next day, November 24, 1883, was a day for great celebration, and not only because the Persson family was all together again.

"Poppa, Momma, hurry! We can't be late for the opening of the Stone Arch Bridge," Fritz called. The family scurried up the seventy-nine wooden plank steps from the river flats and dashed to the entrance of the brand-new bridge crossing the Mississippi River.

"After the steam engine tests out the bridge, we can see each keystone I worked on up close," said Fritz. Every member of the Persson family smiled broadly as James J. Hill inspected and declared the bridge "firmer than the earth which supports it."

"Let's start here, Momma. See the fossil and the pyramid? And there's the Roman arch and the eagle feather. Where is that North Star and the wheat stalk I told you about? Oh, there they are. See, Momma? And way down there is the best one of all. I worked on this one every chance I could all summer long, dreaming of this day when I could show it to my family." Fritz pointed to a heart-shaped key with a capital "P" he had carefully chiseled on one strong keystone of the Stone Arch Bridge.

Vintage Nut Goodie label, Pearson Candy Co.

Author's Note

WHEN MY SON WAS BORN IN 1982, WE NAMED HIM Per, after my grandpa who emigrated from Sweden to Minneapolis. My grandpa became famous in our family as the founder of Pearson Candy Company, the maker of Nut Goodies—a Minnesota treat for over one hundred years.

That same year, my mom compiled our family's story as a gift for her four grandchildren. She began with this quote from *Growing Up* by Russell Baker: "We all come from the past, and children ought to know what it was that went into their making."

Today I am more grateful to my mom for writing down her story than I was in 1982, for it planted the seed for me to write *Keystones of the Stone Arch Bridge*. She included details such as "they left for the dream of plenty in America, as did 33 percent of Sweden's population from 1840 to 1910." And the journey took three weeks in a "terrible old boat." And my grandma Car-

The author's mom, Marion Pearson, marching in the
St. Paul Winter Carnival parade, 1938.

oline (whom I am named after) was almost dropped
overboard at only two years old by her uncle Nils "at
one dramatic moment." (That would've made for an
abrupt ending to my family's story!) They made their
way to Minnesota, "where all the Swedes headed,"
and settled first at the river flats. My mom interjected
that as an art student at the University of Minnesota,

she was assigned to go down to the flats "to sketch the dilapidated, old cottages, never dreaming that [her] roots were there."

You're supposed to write what you know. Over the last ten years, I have been immersed in the panorama view of the Stone Arch Bridge spanning the Mississippi River below St. Anthony Falls. Of course, any bridge can be a significant metaphor in and of itself. Don't we all have that "other side" we want to reach? But a bridge with twenty-three Roman arches, each solidified by a keystone—extraordinary!

The keystones set my imagination ablaze as I learned about the history of the site. When I came upon a photo of a stonecutting crew from 1882, I knew

Stone Arch Bridge stonecutting crew, 1882. MHS

Handstands at the flats.
Courtesy of Hennepin County Library Special Collections

I had a main character to help me tell the story. There in the middle of twenty burly, stern men sat a much younger, earnest-looking worker. It was "Fritz" staring back at me!

Other photos from the 1880s, such as one of children playing on the river flats, helped me embellish Fritz's personality. Perhaps he wasn't always so serious?

One keystone was paramount to the story. Fritz needed a friend who could share the traditions of the first people who lived at the falls, long before there were any bridges. "Margaret," whose great-grandmother was a member of the Red Lake Band and whose Grandpa Bottineau was one of the founders of

St. Anthony, fit the bill. Wanting to add to the fictional Margaret's personality, I found a photo of her older cousin. Marie was a member of the Turtle Mountain Band. She became an attorney, graduating from the Washington College of Law in 1914. The college hon-

Marie Louise Bottineau Baldwin, 1914.
George Grantham Bain Collection, Library of Congress

ored her with a scholarship established in her name. It did, indeed, seem that Margaret could become Fritz's smart friend!

"The Black Community in Territorial St. Anthony: A Memoir" by Emily O. Goodridge Grey revealed how Emily might converse with Fritz. Here's Emily in her own words: "There has not been a moment in my life when I regretted that my feet had touched the soil of Minnesota."

Sometimes research took me to an actual place, even a cemetery called the Minneapolis Pioneer and Soldiers Cemetery on Lake Street at Cedar Avenue. I found the tombstone of Toussaint Grey, the first African American baby to be born in St. Anthony in 1859. He shared this tombstone with his uncle Glenalvin Goodridge, who founded the photography studio in Pennsylvania that Emily told Fritz about as she wove her tales.

One primary source came as a complete surprise. Recently, I examined the deed to the land where my family built our home on Black Oaks Lane west of Minneapolis. There were many names of people who had owned the land, but my gaze hovered over the third entry. It read, "Emily O. Grey, Aug. 31, 1859." And further down it was recorded, "Emily O. Grey and Ralph T. Grey, husband, to Elias Frick, Mar. 24, 1883." My land was once her land! Just like Pierre Bottineau, who is called the founding father of many towns in Minnesota, Grey invested in many acres of land and sold them for a profit. When I look up at the towering, two-hundred-year-old oaks on my lot, I picture Emily Goodridge Grey perhaps doing the same.

The most important keystone for Fritz was the one where he carved his momma's key, for that was his hard-fought goal, to reunite his family. On the next page, you'll see a photograph of Fritz's family at an earlier time. There's Fritz on the left, his poppa and momma in the middle, and his sisters, Hannah and little Inge. At the top right is his older brother, Per Edward, the founder of Pearson Candy Company in 1909. He was my grandpa. Fritz's family is my family!

This story is dedicated to all the families who have bridged the mighty Mississippi at the site of its most powerful waterfall.

Fritjof's family

Glossary

Boozhoo is an Ojibwe greeting invoking the great teacher, Nanabozho.

A **cauldron** is a large kettle or pot for boiling.

A **chisel** is a metal tool with a cutting-edge blade, used to chip away or shape stone; a **mallet** is a hammer with a barrel-shaped head used for tapping on the chisel.

A **cord** is a stack of wood measuring four feet by four feet by eight feet.

Haŋ is the Dakota word for "hello."

Mormor is a Swedish word for grandma on the mother's side of the family.

A **premonition** is a feeling that something is going to happen.

A **quarry** is an open excavation of the ground where workers locate and carve out stones for building.

Quills are the hollow, sharp spines of a porcupine; they are tipped with little hooks called **barbs.**

Tusen tack is a Swedish phrase meaning "a thousand thanks."

The **Underground Railroad** was a vast network of people who helped slaves escape from the South to the northern United States and Canada in the 1850s and 1860s, sometimes by boat or train but usually in a series of safe houses called *stations*.

Valkommen is the Swedish word for "welcome."

A **vardtrad** is a guardian tree planted in the center of the yard of many Swedish homes; caring for the tree shows respect for ancestors.

A **windlass** is a machine for pulling or lifting; it involves a roller on which a rope is wound by a work horse.

A **wooden trough** is a long, shallow container used for drinking water or to feed animals.

Historical Figures

Pierre Bottineau (1817–95) was a voyageur, fur trader, frontier guide, and interpreter. His father was Charles Bottineau, a French Canadian voyageur, and his mother was Mizhakwadookwe or "Clear Sky Woman." Pierre founded many towns in Minnesota.

Emily Goodridge Grey (1834–1916) came to St. Anthony, Minnesota, in 1857 with her son, William, to join her husband, Ralph, a barber. They formed a growing community of African Americans. Her second son, Touissant L'Ouverture Grey, was the first African American child born in St. Anthony. He was named after General Touissant L'Ouverture, the African slave who liberated Haiti from the French and became governor of the island nation. Emily's father, William Goodridge, a freed slave, was active in the Underground Railroad in Philadelphia and later came to live in St. Anthony.

Father Louis Hennepin (1626–1705), a Catholic priest, missionary, and explorer, was sent from Belgium to search for the Mississippi River. He was the first European to see the only waterfall on the Mississippi, which he named St. Anthony Falls.

James J. Hill (1838–1916) was born in Canada and settled in St. Paul, Minnesota, at the age of seventeen. In 1879, he formed a company that eventually became the Great Northern Railway, expanding rail lines to the Pacific Ocean. He became known as the Empire Builder.

Eliza Winston (1830– ?), a thirty-year-old slave, was brought to St. Anthony, Minnesota, in 1860 by Colonel Richard Christmas. Emily and Ralph Grey brought her to court, where she was pronounced free, and she escaped via the Underground Railroad.

An interpreter at Mill City Museum for ten years, **Carolyn Ruff** has owned an art gallery in the Minneapolis Warehouse District, has served as a reading consultant in Minnesota, Japan, and Germany, and celebrates her own Swedish heritage in this, her first book. Photo by Per Ruff.

The FOSSIL

 The PYRAMID

 The ROMAN ARCH

 The EAGLE FEATHER

 The NORTH STAR

 The WHEAT STALK

 The KEY